THE SAGA OF LOVE
VIA TELEPHONE
...tring tring

PANKAJ PANDEY

MAHAVEER PUBLISHERS
New Delhi

Published by
MAHAVEER PUBLISHERS
4764/2A, 23-Ansari Road
Daryaganj, New Delhi – 110002
Ph. : 011 – 66629669–79–89
Fax. : 011 – 41563419
E-mail : mahaveerpublishers@gmail.com

This is a work of fiction. Names, characters, places and incidents are products of the
author's imagination or are used fictitiously and are not to be construed as real. Any
resemblance to actual events, locales, organisations, or persons living or dead, is
entirely coincidental.

First Edition: 2008

ISBN: 81-8352-066-9

Distributed by
VAIBHAV BOOK SERVICE
E-mail : vaibhavbookservice@gmail.com
Web : www.vaibhavbooks.com

Published by D.K. Jha for Mahaveer Publishers
Printed by Chaman Offset Printers, New Delhi

*Dedicated to my
Mom, Dad and Dream*

ACKNOWLEDGEMENT

The Saga of Love via Telephone has been a very special project, brought to fruition through the effort of some very special people. This project reflects my love for my dream. This project was not planned; it just happened because I had to start somewhere.

I am thankful to Kamlesh Pandey, Jitendra Kumar, Rahul Singh and Chandan Jaiswal, who were very much with me in all my doings.

I am grateful to Amalesh Pandey for his invaluable input to this book.

Gratitude is also due to my college buddies and friends— Neha, Pushpendra, Atul Sachan and Shivam Gupta. They may not have directly contributed to the writing or the production of the book, but they have always been there for me whenever I needed them.

I would like to thank the publishing team, especially Manju Gupta, Azeem Ahmad Khan and Dilip Jha for extending unconditional support.

Above all, I am grateful to my parents Chandra Shekher Pandey and Savitri Pandey, my brothers Ranjeet Kumar Pandey and Amitesh Kumar Pandey for the unflinching support they have always provided me to chase my maverick aspirations.

Thanks to the character 'Shikha' who remained an inspiration for me throughout my writings and showed me the way.

Dream is not what you see in sleep...
Dream is the thing which does not let you sleep...!

—Dr A.P.J. Abdul Kalam

A Word or Two....

Life is not a bed of roses; it is nothing short of a struggle. We fight for something or the other every day. The society acts as a catalyst in all our doings. It's upon us to believe in our self and in the person who trusts us and vice versa.

There is a tide in affairs of all people;
when taken at the right time, it leads to fortune.

It simply means that it is we who decide our future and nobody else. Everything which we possess is due to our efforts. Let me tell you a story.

A donkey, a father and a son went on a journey, each trudging along at his own speed. Two passers-by said: "How foolish they are! Can't they ride astride the donkey?"

So, the next day, the father sat on the donkey and the son continued walking. Again some passers-by remarked, "See, the father is so shameless! He himself is sitting on the donkey and is not bothered about his son, who is being made to walk in this scorching heat of the sun."

Next day, the son rode the donkey while the father walked. The passers-by remarked, "Just witness this strange sight. The father must have brought up his child with great love and care. But, see, the child is riding astride the donkey, while the father is walking. How shameless the son is! Can't he allow his father to sit on the donkey?"

On the final day of the journey, both father and son sat on the donkey, hoping that this way they would escape further comments. But the passers-by said: "It's ludicrous! There is no humanity left in the world. Both father and son are sitting comfortably on the donkey. It seems as if the donkey will collapse soon."

People in this world can never appreciate you, no matter what you do.

If you try to avoid any situation instead of facing it boldly, it will only invite a bigger situation which will be more fierce, more difficult to handle.

Hence, confront life, no matter what it brings, believing in yourself and trusting those who trust you.

Happy reading!

Pankaj Pandey
(*oscarsindia@yahoo.com*)

CONTENTS

1

Novice Lover

Self-kindled every atom glows,
and hints the future which it owes.

— Ralph Waldo Emerson

She emerged through the lane from her classroom with open hair, a tinge of lip-liner, walking next to hundreds of students, some standing right in her path. Without getting perturbed, she walked across the lawn, went to the library, returned her books and walked back on the same path before disappearing out of sight.

It was amazing...

I had never seen a girl behave in such a different manner.

That night, while I was studying, she unknowingly entered my mind, preventing me from completing my task.

Those were unforgettable moments and I was impressed by her.

Next day, when I went to college, my eyes searched for her in the crowd. I didn't even tell my friends about this as they would have ridiculed me. I never let anyone know that I had noticed a girl, who had left an indelible impression on my mind.

I would often analyse the way she walked and also her style of keeping the tippet round her neck. Her lips shone as if they were reflections of champagne. Sharp features on her face held me transfixed. I loved to hear the sound of her anklets when she passed by. She was admirable.

A uniform was prescribed in our college and she dressed in such a way that none would fail to notice her. She had a very pleasant nature.

She often came to the first floor to collect some stationery items and I would intently gaze at her as my classroom was on the first floor.

I was a boy with good looks, lean of build and of fair complexion. If marks in class were the hallmark of a good student, then I was one, but she was better than me.

She lived in a private hostel while I lived in Engineers Palace (the name of our rented flat). The Engineers Palace had five permanent residents: Pankaj (me), Anurag, Ritesh, Amit and Sujeet. If the first alphabet of each name was to be arranged one after another, it read as PARAS. We had such a lively and friendly nature that many of our other friends wished to live a life like us.

Anurag was a friend of Shikha. Within ten days of my love at first sight, I had started mailing her on Orkut. For the first six days I did not receive any reply. But I was not the one to be easily disheartened. I continued to mail her at regular intervals till she was forced to enquire about me. I just wanted to be noticed by her.

But she was too practical a girl. My other friend, Shreya, was close to her and lived in the same hostel.

She told Shikha as to what kind of person I was and all that she knew about my behaviour and nature. In the meantime, she accepted my desire for friendship via the Orkut site.

Even a slightest success in love makes a person feel
as if he has conquered a planet.

I was a desperate sort of guy; despite possessing a lot of self-confidence, I was impatient to talk to her. I used to check my scraps regularly to see if she had sent any reply or not.

During college days I was a fairly talented as I used to participate in all kinds of competitions and had won some fairly good prizes.

Our semester results were declared and I fared well in the examination but, as usual, she secured a better percentage. She was jubilant and I was exhilarated. Then came February 14, Valentines Day—the day I was desperately waiting for. The Air Force written examination results had been declared and I qualified in it. I thought it would be the best time to talk to her, so I dialled her number and began, "Hi Shikha, this is Pankaj."

"Hi," she replied in a vibrant tone.

"You know, I have qualified in the Air Force written examination," I announced proudly.

"Oh, that's great! Congratulations. When are you offering me a treat?" she asked.

"Very soon," I replied.

Her voice was comparable to that of a nightingale—it was so sweet! On hearing her voice, I felt I had lost my senses and was flying high up in the sky.

Next day, when I saw her in college, she was surrounded by her friends. I waved my hand and she responded alike, but in a subdued manner so that nobody would catch her gesture.

I was happy that she had responded to my overtures. Now, my dream was to continue with the relationship, whatever it was. So, I gathered feedback by talking to some of her close friends. I found that she was impressed by me. I was, however, reluctant to call her again.

Without fail, I would daily think about her but could not muster the courage to talk to her. After eight days, I dialled her number. We talked as if we had known each other for long. I don't know what she liked in me—my optimistic nature, I presume! We talked about our friends, their characteristics, shared same jokes, guided each other on how to proceed in life and shape our career and everything else possible under the sun. The duration of our talk used to be long. This helped me believe that she too liked me.

I started talking to her daily. Numerous questions arose in my mind on how to proceed—whether she would understand me or not, what to talk about and so on. Finally I left everything to destiny to decide our fate.

It was a Monday when I rang her in the evening. She sounded a bit nervous and tense as though she was troubled in mind. She was surrounded by many of her friends 'waiting for their lovers', as she used to say.

I knew everything about her (her past, her present), but she was unaware about the sense of excitement that used to engulf me every time I talked to her. I used to be so happy that it cannot be expressed on paper. Shikha was really quixotic!

As days passed, we became more familiar and started understanding each other better. She began to trust me and shared a few of her past secrets in life. She told me about a guy who was her friend since the past few years. The man had a fierce attitude and a lethal nature that kept him involved in all kinds of activities that did not impress the kind of girl Shikha was.

Being curious by nature, I began to realise how innocent and sober she was. Her voice was so sweet. I was so much preoccupied in listening to her that I did not catch the gravity of the situation in which she was. After an hour or so, when I realised the seriousness, I gave her a suggestion, "Why don't you lodge a police complaint if he is pestering you? That will prevent him from calling you again and again. He will not dare to disturb you then."

She was not satisfied by my suggestion and said, "I will not entertain him and will change my number."

However, it has been my firm conviction that all good actions are bound to bear fruit.

When our conversation got over, I realised that I too had some rigid streak in me about which she would be able to learn in few days. After meeting Shikha, I had decided to amend my ways. I would rather say that I gradually started spreading my tentacles in love.

2

Understanding Love

For the experience of each new age requires a new confession, and the world seems always waiting for its poet.

— **Ralph Waldo Emerson**

It was Sunday. The sun was shining gloriously as if wishing me good luck. I had to visit my brother's place. So, I rang up Shikha early in the morning and said, "Listen, Shikha, I may not be able to call you for a day or two."

A moment or two of shocked silence ensued.

After a few moments, she asked, "Why?"

I told her about my programme. "I will call you as soon as I arrive," I said.

Noticing that it was getting late, she quickly bade me adieu.

It was my first visit to my brother's house after my love at first sight. The whole day I spent with my brother, shopping in Lajpat Nagar market and buying trousers, shirts, etc. though my mind never left Shikha. She was not near me but I was with her every moment. I had decided that she had made a great impact on my life and it would not be easy for me to lead a life without her in future. I decided to completely 'whitewash' myself and fill myself in the colours she liked. I started amending my traits which I felt she would not like as I believed that renunciation without aversion cannot be lasting.

I hurried back as soon as possible to talk to my first love. Being an optimist by nature, I have always believed in doing things and achieving success. I also believe that if a person performs some action for fulfilling some purpose and is not motivated by prejudice, then he is bound to achieve success. The law of doing any activity is inexorable and impossible to evade.

My brother had asked me to go on an important assignment which meant being out of station. 'Should I say no?' I asked myself. It would really be impossible to disobey him. 'God help me out, please. How do I get out of this situation?' I thought.

Suddenly an idea clicked in my mind. 'Important topics are left for tomorrow. If I miss those, it will not be easy for me to cover up,' I thought.

While returning, I went to a bookstall. I was in search of a book which would help me in understanding girls—their worries, anxiety, enthusiasm, what they liked and what they hated most in boys. I went to 'Crossword' where such books are easily available. I searched for the right book in every row with my keen eyes and managed to shortlist about ten books from different shelves. 'But which would be worth buying?' I wondered! I finally decided to consult the shopkeeper.

"Which among these will help in understanding girls better?" I asked him enthusiastically.

He rejected all the books of my choice and pointed his finger at a green-coloured book kept in the middle row of the miscellaneous section.

I went near the shelf and took out the book, turning over the pages with curiosity.

It read: *Men are from Mars, Women are from Venus.* I briefly went through some paragraphs. The wall-clock sounded ten times. 'Oh, heck! It's too late. I am late.' It was 11.15 p.m. when I reached Engineers Palace.

I love Anurag. He may not be a genius, but he has always been a good roommate, a loyal friend and a kind senior. He possessed the knack for flirting, making friends and waiting for girls outside their houses, just in front of their windows so that he could catch a glimpse of them.

It could be said he was a true friend indeed.

Anurag was an endearing friend, attracting a number of proposals from all kinds of quarters. His interest, however, lay in becoming a software professional.

"Genuine software professional," he would say.

"The telephone has been entertaining us since 7 o'clock," said Anurag. "More than twenty calls have come but no one has attended to those calls," he added.

I had asked my friends not to attend the call of a specific number.

I was crouching by the chair. I dialled her number. It was 12 o'clock. My heart would start beating faster if she took some time to attend the call.

"Were you sleeping?" I asked.

"Yeah."

"Okay, no problem," I said.

I began to imagine her, looking utterly beautiful while asleep—she had the looks to participate in any beauty pageant.

"Tell me, why did you make a number of phone calls to me in my absence?" I asked in an insane manner.

"I felt like talking," she replied, showing her own generosity of spirit.

"Talking to whom?" I asked.

"You, idiot."

"Thanks for the compliment, Ma'am."

A shocked silence ensued; not even the humming of bees was audible. The distance separating us must have been 5 kilometres, but I felt as though she sat 5 inches away from me.

"Now, should I let you sleep or..." I added, in an enquiring tone, as if prompting her to say something to me.

"You can continue talking. I am listening as well as replying," she said.

A wave of happiness passed through my veins. After some time, I felt as if she had fallen into deep slumber. So I wished her goodnight. There was no reply.

At times we felt extremely happy and at times, deeply sad. If only we could cultivate the art of savouring every moment of life for the unexpected challenges it brings, then life could become extraordinarily happy. It is the law of nature—when there is interest, we feel exuberant; but when there is no interest, life seems mechanical and ordinary.

The next day I was late in waking up. However, I attended to my daily ablutions and reached college as early as possible. I was 25 minutes late. It was 9.25 a.m.

The teacher showed no change in expression, for it had become my daily routine to reach late. I could never attend my first class on time, though I always dreamt to be punctual.

The environment in the college seemed different, somehow unusual. It was not that the fragrance of the flowers intoxicated me or that some disco show was to be organised which had sent my spirits soaring; but, something was different.

We had to appear for a pool campus interview. Everybody seemed excited. I had been preparing for the interview from the past seven to ten days. Moreover, I had thought I would not get a better chance to impress her. It was the last working day before the official holiday for Holi festival. What if 'I were to get selected?' I thought!

"Will it impress her?" I asked Amit.

"Of course, it will," he replied.

"To get selected at this stage would add colour to your love. Your image will rise in her eyes," he added.

Shikha had once told me she liked intelligent guys and that she would consider marrying a guy who was good at his studies, earned a lot of money and who loved her a lot.

Possibly, Shikha was a materialistic girl.

But that hardly mattered to me. I considered it futile to try to glean information on the true values of her mind. When I dialled her phone to convey this news, she was busy packing her clothes, as she was going home the next day. In any case, she was aware of the recruitment drive. I was exuberant at the campus drive but sad that she was leaving the city. As I had to prepare for the interview, I quickly bade her goodbye.

3

Love-catalysing Engineer

Success is a lousy teacher. It seduces smart people into thinking they can't lose.

—**Bill Gates**

But one thing certainly energised me, it was her saying, "Go big or stay home. Nothing is small. Start from small and reach to the top."

I must say, Shikha was a great motivator.

My friends-cum-roommates were leaving for their hometowns. Ritesh, Sujeet and Anurag—all had left, leaving behind Amit and me. "I have to clear the interview; I am left with no alternative," I said to Amit.

"You will do that, Champ. I have full faith in you. But for now, you must be mentally prepared," he replied.

I prepared the whole night so as to be successful in the interview. It is always better to judge the seriousness of a situation rather than to repent later. Amit had left his chair at 2.00 a.m., but I continued to sit till 4.00 a.m. I had set the alarm clock for 6.00 a.m. as we had to reach by 8 a.m. and the collage was a fair distance away from Engineers Palace.

But, as usual, we woke up at 7 o'clock. "Get up, it's already seven," Amit said, shaking me awake.

I woke up in a hurry. It was a day to perform; perform to win.

Since Shikha was with me, I felt I was in a win-win situation.

Though in a tearing hurry, I could not prevent myself from dialling Shikha's telephone number.

"Good morning," I said in such a way as if I was hosting a radio show. The voice was loud and clear.

"Haven't you left yet? It's already 7.30," she said, in a surprised tone.

"How could I leave before wearing some snazzy clothes," I joked.

"Oh God! Help him. Are you going for a disco?" she asked in mocking anger.

"I can think over that. Will you accompany me?" I bantered.

"Stop this lousy crap," she said sternly. "C'mon Pankaj, be serious. Now, wear some smart clothes and leave as early as possible."

"Which shade (colour) should I prefer?" I asked.

"Which are the colours you have?"

I gave her a list of them.

She took some time and then suggested a unique combination. "Why don't you try that parrot coloured shirt and chocolate coloured trousers? You dazzle in that combination."

"Okay, Ma'am, as you wish," I said happily.

"Now, no more talking. Are you leaving or should I disconnect?" she threatened.

"You know, I don't like that," I replied.

"Yeah, I know."

"But I am doing it for you. All the best." There was a long beep sound.

I believe that one falls is love when the mind is somewhere between doubt and certainty. While our phone talk was going on, I saw Amit laughing, muttering and obviously, teasing me.

"This guy is no less than mad," he murmured. "Now, should we leave? It's already 8.30," he said agitatedly.

After some time we left for the venue.

It was 9.30 a.m. when we reached the centre.

There was no tension, no frustration! We were both equally happy. Our mood of exhilaration made it seem as if we were out on a safari.

Amit was a multi-natured guy. He was a 'legitimate' guy— legitimate is the only word in the dictionary which can best describe him. He was a good motivator, good advisor and a good human being. Never known to be a high thinker, he was always target-oriented. He was blunt but had a lively and cheerful nature. He stood by me in all my triumphs and failures, ensuring my success in every form and in all aspects of life.

The crowd at the centre was nearly around 2,500. Everybody was yelling at the top of his voice for the hall-ticket.

We were made to sit in different classrooms, around thirty in each. There were two sets of paper. I was confident that I would be able to get through the papers without any hitch.

That very evening, the result was declared. I was engrossed in admiring the scenic beauty, busy in one of the malls. Unaware of the result, I reached Engineers Palace late at night.

"Hey Pankaj, you have been selected. Gear up for the interview tomorrow," announced Amit, my admirer. He even hugged me.

My initial desire was to share the news with my parents but, on second thought, I decided to spring a surprise on them at my final selection.

Calls from my numerous well-wishers poured in. I felt different that day.

But Shikha was uppermost on my mind, so, I dialled her number.

"All channels are busy. Please dial after some time," was the reply.

'Hey Shikha! Where are you?' I thought, I tried again but the message was same.

I must have tried at least fifty times when something struck my mind that sent me preparing for the next-day interview.

I studied the whole night, looked for every detail, squeezed through previous questions, thus ensuring that no loop-hole was left in my preparation. I prepared hard, so hard that I could not be subdued by any damn question.

The whole night passed without sleeping. Next morning, before leaving for the venue, I dialled her number.

"Hi, Shikha! It's me. You know, I have accumulated all the possible questions within my mighty brain."

"Congratulations," she said. She was very happy. I could feel her happiness. "Okay then, today is your interview."

I was in a state of dilemma whether to ask her or not, then, finally I asked, "Did you switch off your mobile last night?" I asked, hesitatingly.

"No. I didn't," she replied.

"You know, Shikha, I tried your number several times last night to give you this news, but the line was busy."

"Oh God! But that's not my mistake," she laughed. "We waited for about six hours for our train. We have just arrived home," she said. "Anyway, rush for your interview."

"Okay, pay my regards to Mom and Dad," I said.

After our conversation it was clear to me that today nobody could overrun me. I could not be subdued by anyone.

The venue for the interview was the same as that for the test. So, I reached the centre on time for the first time.

We were called one by one, according to our college numbers.

A mixture of confidence and nervousness was apparent in my behaviour. I was waiting for my turn to come when suddenly... "Pankaj Kumar, Room No. 9."

So Room No. 9 was to decide my fate. I was a bit nervous, my heart pounded fast. As I wanted to boost my confidence, I concentrated on Shikha's words, when she had said, "*A dream can be nurtured over years and years and then flourish rapidly. Be patient. It will happen for you. Sooner or later, life will get weary of beating on you and holding the door shut on you. Then it will let you in and throw you a real party.*"

I was filled with confidence. The interviewer was man of about fifty-five years of age.

His eyes stared at me. I thought he was deaf as he not even once laughed or shook head when I responded to his razor-sharp questions. He asked me about everything—from personal to professional, from national to international and from politics to sports.

While answering his questions I tried to behave in such a way that he would be impressed by my confidence, diligence, eloquence and intelligence. Anyways, the interview, which lasted for about 45 minutes got over, and my only worry was to get selected.

After the interview, scores of students surrounded me. "What questions were asked?" Shivam asked.

I told him everything, right from length to breadth.

He had envisaged the pattern of interview and prepared himself for the task. Shivam, a friend of mine, was a talented, multi-cultured and a capable guy. Multi-cultured, because he did his schooling from schools of different states.

I had to pack my bags and rush to the station. Abhisekh, one of my classmates-cum-friend, also accompanied me.

While returning from the centre, we visited a temple as Abhisekh thought that this act would bring us laurels.

Now, we (Abhisekh and I) decided on a meeting place, before taking a conveyance and rushing to the station. In the meantime some of our friends had also joined us.

"Ritu and Manish have missed their train," Abhisekh said. "They would be going with us," he added.

My attention was far from his words as I was desperately waiting for the results. I had asked Shivam to contact me as soon as the results were to be declared.

Suddenly I remarked, "No problem. I mean it's good."

I saw an insidious smile on his face.

I could see a long line of wooden houses with children in front and a few scraggly trees from the window of my moving train. After some time, I joined my friends who were sitting in another compartment. Whatever be the circumstances, the subject of discussion had to be one of universal interest—entertainment.

Finally we reached the New Delhi railway station from where we had to board another train.

"It's 5.30 p.m. One hour left," announced Manish.

Suddenly...

"*Doston ki dosti, yaron ki yari kam lagne lagi, behke-behke hum hein, yeh sama hai...*" It was the ringing tone of my mobile phone. 'Shivam calling,' it read.

Without losing a fraction of a second, I received the call. "We have been selected," a voice thundered in my ears.

I was no longer is my senses. It was an exuberant overture for me.

Some of my friends had also been selected. When I passed this message to my brother, who also accompanied me for the journey, he patted me on my back. I tried Shikha's number several times, but failed as there was some network congestion problem.

Meanwhile, we celebrated our success with Cokes in the compartment. We were in a jubilant mood, with my friends demanding a grand party.

My brother and I reached Renukoot, our home-town, the next morning. Everybody was happy to receive the news. It was party time.

4

Enjoying Holidays

The world is full of judgement days, and into every assembly that a man enters, in every action he attempts, he is gauged and stamped.

—Ralph Waldo Emerson

Amidst all the celebrations, an important corner of my mind was concentrated upon Shikha.

I called her late in the evening on a replacement number which she had given for contacting her during her stay in her home-town. I dialled that number with the mild hope that she would receive the call.

"Hello!" It was a strange voice for me. It was the voice of her mother.

So after the usual exchange of banalities, I asked in a shaky voice, "Is Shikha there?"

"No, she is not," she volleyed back.

I could not gather the courage to enquire where she was. Without waiting for a fraction of a second, she disconnected the call.

I could not sleep that entire night. My thoughts revolved round her and our undisclosed love. I was as desperate to talk to her as a traveller would be for water in the midst of a desert.

Her mother was orthodox and the grey matter which filled her skull was old and traditional, I believed. In the subsequent days, however, Shikha told me that her mother was sizing me up, as also my demeanour and accent. Mothers usually do it if the boy has anything to do with their daughter.

"Good morning, son."

"Good morning, father," I replied.

"It seems you haven't slept last night. Were you upset?"

"No, nothing of the sort. Actually, an insect bit my eye, so, it's swollen red," I replied.

I have always been close to my father and could share everything with him. But, how could I share this with him as I had yet to go a long way. 'What if he were to scold me?' I thought. All such questions haunted me.

I decided not to say anything to my father. During daytime, I was busy in regular home affairs.

But, around 7.15 p.m., I dialled Shikha's number and asked, "Is Shikha there?" without bothering to find who was on the receiving side.

"Hello, Shikha here."

"Hi Shikha!" I said. "Yet another success."

"Congratulations," she remarked. It was this reply which seemed like the real award I was waiting for. "Who else?" she enquired.

I gave a list of names.

"Okay, bye," she said and disconnected the call without waiting for a second. I felt humiliated as to how she could do like this to me! 'Is this the way to disconnect my call,' I thought. I had a strange sinking feeling. My mobile rang just then.

"Hey Pankaj, I was surrounded by my family members so I could not talk much."

"It's okay."

"I am so happy; I need a treat," she said.

My father was standing in front of me, searching for some papers.

"Thank God, he has left," I said, in a relieved manner.

"What happened?" She enquired.

"Nothing, my father was here in search of something," I replied.

"You know, Pankaj, I was sure of your success and I am also sure you will go a long way in life. I don't know you much, else I would have easily said that you are the best."

Our conversation continued for the next half an hour.

My sister, who knew about her, enquired about our conversation. I gave her a convincing answer and she was relieved.

We could not talk every day during our holidays, but she had been in my thoughts for every single second that I stayed with my parents. It was my conviction that in this mundane existence she would never lead me astray and would always confide to me her innermost thoughts. I could notice that we were drawing closer day by day. I knew a number of girls but she was above them all. She was a treat for my eyes and ears; an angel for me. I was even terrified of ever hurting her feelings.

Days passed and so did weeks and months.

She was leaving for the city (our rendezvous) when I called her. She said her sister was keen to talk to me. Meanwhile she said, "I will be there in a week's time."

"I got to do some urgent work," I said.

"Okay, dear," she replied.

My family and I visited my uncle's place on the occasion of his daughter's marriage. There was lot of fun and excitement. I could get to meet some eminent members of our large family. It was a delight to meet them after a long time.

A number of rituals are performed on marriage occasions and on the scheduled day, I was watching each of them very carefully and enjoying myself.

Every ritual performed carried my thoughts to Shikha and 'our love'. While the rest were busy in the festivities, I dialled her number.

"When are you coming, man?" she enquired.

"It will take another three to four days," I replied. "What are you doing?"

"We are chilling out in the market."

"You and...," I stopped.

"Shreya. What did you think? Brad Pitt," she laughed.

I could feel her enjoying. Shreya was a common friend of ours. She was an obdurate sort of girl, with a quiet nature. She always seemed lost in her world. She was blunt to the core. In real sense she was a 'scrounge'. Anyway, she was good to me and more importantly, she was an advisor and well-wisher of Shikha. They were good friends who shared every minute detail of their past and daily affairs. So, both were enjoying ice-cream in the market! 'Choco-berry, I guess, is her favourite.'

"Pankaj, aunt is calling you," a voice echoed.

"Coming."

"Okay Shikha, I got to keep the receiver down."

"Bye, take care of yourself," she replied.

When I came down the stairs from the balcony, I saw almost everybody swinging their hips to the music. Everybody was dancing and enjoying.

I too joined them and the party rocked. Now, came the final day, that is, the day of the marriage. Everybody had chosen a dress of their choice; for me it was one of Shikha's choice. I don't know whether I dazzled in that combination but then, to think of this was almost out of question. Amidst a number of traditional rituals the procession wound its way and as usual the 'crying ceremony'—the departure of the bride, was in full progress.

I have never liked tears in the eyes of anybody. I cannot see them, specially in girls and women. So, I went away from there.

Finally. the day of my departure came. I boarded the train for the city. Everybody was sad, except me. I cannot explain what kind of joy filled me as my people wished me goodbye.

Hours passed and I reached the city.

5

Augmenting Love

After the final no, comes a yes, and on that yes the future world depends.

—Wallace Stevens

I had reached Engineers Palace.

Knock, knock!

It was Sujeet who opened the door. He was in the city after a gap of one complete month. After long, the Engineers Palace was complete with all its five engineers present in it.

"Hey Sujeet, how are you man?"

"I am fine. What about you?" he retorted. "How is your love affair going."

"It's not going; it's flying."

"Oh, that's great," he sounded thrilled.

"On seeing you it becomes clear that love makes life worth living," he remarked.

I met all my friends who were waiting to see me. Someone else was also waiting, but I decided to meet her later.

We giggled and enjoyed as we shared our experiences. It was amazing how our friends are always with us and we can share everything with them. Sujeet, 'the mordant boy' as we used to call him, had a helping nature. He was true from his heart, not bothered about tomorrow and casual in approach. We called him 'mordant' because he used to make us laugh with his sarcastic remarks. The environment at the Engineers Palace was always lively and happening.

I had great plans ahead. In the evening when I dialled to talk to Shikha, she shot back, "Welcome back. When did you arrive?"

"Yesterday," I said.

"And, you are calling me now?" she volleyed back.

"I got stuck in some work, so I could not contact you," I replied.

"Okay, then, what's up?"

"Nothing, you know..." I stopped.

"No, I don't know. How can I know unless you tell me?" She was a 'regale' in the real sense.

"I like you. I mean I like everything about you. Your lively nature, cool attitude, friendly behaviour, everything."

"Hey, I have a lot of negative qualities," she added while trying to cross-check me.

"You are a human being. You are bound to have some negative qualities, else you will be God; but it hardly matters how many negative qualities you have. What matters is, I like you. Do you like me?" I asked .

"Yeah, I do. That's why I talk to you." She gave me a list of my qualities which she categorised into two, though it's my conviction that I don't have a marked or defined positive and negative quality. Some of my negative qualities become positive depending on the circumstances and vice-versa.

I deeply admired her nature and told her so. "As a child, my parents had taught me not to hurt anybody's feelings and I adhere to this philosophy even now," she said. "I believe we are all here for a short time, so why not make the best of what we have."

With more than seventy hours of discussions (till that date) that I had held so far with her, I felt that this was her strength and forte.

My voice used to dip low whenever I enquired how much she like me. I would be worried that what would I do, if she were to say 'no'.

I loved her so much that I wanted my day to start by seeing her and end in a similar way. But it was not possible. Somehow, I managed to start and end the day by hearing her voice.

Meanwhile, my friend's demand for a grand party could not be delayed, so a date was decided upon.

Each one of us decked ourselves to the best in swanky clothes, cool hair-style and funky looks. We were six in number; Chandan, a close friend, also accompanied us.

We went to an old restaurant where everybody ordered what they wanted. There was no restriction, at all. Just a second...

Cocktails were prohibited. Shikha didn't like alcohol and neither had I taken a sip of it ever.

Everybody was enjoying. One of us ordered a cockle. It was a new dish for me. Everything looked complete except for one—she was not with us. How could she be? It was 10 p.m. and the warden did not allow girls to go out at that ungodly hour.

Meanwhile, the party was in full swing. Well, telling lousy jokes was the main attraction of the party, not to forget the sizzling curries which we had ordered. Everybody watched us as we were the cynosure of all those present in the restaurant. I can only say, 'Boys are boys.'

The bill came—it was more than a student could afford. It was 11.30 p.m. when we returned to Engineers Palace.

"Four missed calls. One is from your father and the next three from Shikha," said Ritesh.

My father is the best Dad that God could have ever made. According to him, I was the rose of his garden. In his words—'I was invincible and inviolable.'

During my conversation with my father, he enquired about my well-being and my studies, advising me to study with my full heart and mind. How could I tell him that my heart was filled with Shikha's love and there was hardly any space left for studies!

Since we all were very tired, we were half asleep when my telephone rang.

"Hello," I said in a sleepy voice.

"Are you sleeping?" she enquired.

"Yeah," I said.

"Anyway, how was the party?"

"It was nice. There were lots of girls in the restaurant."

"And you liked them," she said, pulling my leg in jest.

"Hey, how do you know that?"

There was a strange silence.

"C'mon, Shikha. I like you. I was merely kidding."

Days passed and we started drawing closer to each other. The examination dates were announced and engineers at Engineers Palace got busy in preparing for them, except for me. I had manoeuvred my move and was convinced that if executed perfectly, it would work. I could not afford to lose her at any cost. I don't know why I was so cautious! Was it love or was it an exception? I had no answers and I didn't want either.

She used to keep a fast on every Saturday. When I enquired about the reason for doing so, she replied, "I have kept a fast since I was in Standard V. Many-a-times, my mother has scolded me but I have never left the practice."

She used to cook well and some recipes were her favourite. "I am no voracious eater but I like spicy food."

Do you know how one feels when a boy gets a girlfriend who possesses every quality that he likes? I too don't know, because it cannot be explained in words but I felt so every moment.

Shikha told me that she was adept at preparing tea and her friends pestered her to prepare tea.

After all, these friends tend to send you high up in the sky and then pull you down by your legs for fun. Anyway, one day she told me how to prepare a 'special tea'. She told me the recipe.

I was not a novice at this recipe, but she had a different style of preparing it.

I was least interested in hearing but I was forced to hear. You could never tell when these girls may get annoyed. So, it was better to be careful.

At later stages, I tried to follow her recipe and it really tasted nice. Her style of telling things was perfect. Nobody could copy her, I felt. Meanwhile, we used to compliment each other seriously for what all we had done during school and this involved a galore of giggles. I must admit she was a great entertainer.

She could narrate various things about her family, their likes and dislikes, her past; but never about her future. She had no vivid future plans! All she wanted was a safe job and nothing more than to feel safe and secure.

While I, on my part, loved innovative new ideas, explored new things and pushed the envelope beyond its capabilities. That was all because I considered myself an entrepreneur from both my heart and mind.

.I have always appreciated people like Albert Einstein, Mahatma Gandhi and countless others who did not strive to be different, but were different because they thought different. They always made the choice to contribute something meaningful and thus stood tall despite the chaos and anger surrounding them.

Then, came the best night of my life—a night about which I had never dreamt. I rang her up around 9.00 p.m. She was in a foul mood because of the food served in her hostel. "Today I went mad," she said.

"Thank God. Somehow you realised this," I teased.

"Stop the lousy crap. It really annoys me," she continued.

"Okay tell, what happened?" I enquired.

"Only a mad person can eat the kind of food that is served in our hostel; especially what was served today. The owner is so profit-conscious; so cheap."

"So, what did you do?"

"No dinner," she replied.

"You must be hungry; lets go to a restaurant."

"It's not needed. I had some fruits and it's already 10.30 p.m."

We were on our twenty-second orbit round the sun, but this was such juvenile behaviour. During my school days I was famous for cracking jokes. So, I managed to cool her down by talking to her incessantly of all kinds of things. If a third person had heard our talk, he would have considered us mad.

Being of a caring nature, she asked me about my daily and specific routines. We talked for hours and hours. It was 1.00 a.m. when she said, "I am feeling sleepy. Should I sleep now?"

"No, continue for some more time," I begged.

"Okay, then wait for a minute. I need to go upstairs to the balcony." She narrated numerous jokes and I felt as if I was on a trek of stars in the sky.

"Wow, Zephyr," she shouted.

"And......"

"Many stars are twinkling in the sky."

"And......"

"Everybody else is sleeping except me."

"And..."

"And these mosquitoes are biting me. Mummy..." she shrieked.

"Has your Mummy arrived or what?" I laughed.

"No-oo-o... these mosquitoes. This world would have been more beautiful if these mosquitoes had not been there. Is there any need for these mosquitoes?" She was sitting on the floor of the balcony. "You know, the colour of my skin is changing. It's becoming red," she added

"Why?" I enquired.

'Cause you are an oaf and these mosquitoes..." She had a way of disparaging me even while uttering laudatory phrases.

When I enquired, she said, "I know you are on cloud nine, but the real winner is one who can actually sustain his success. I would like to see you high up in the sky—so high that with every passing moment your lustre waxes. In my rarest of rare desires I would never like anything to wane your success rate. "Okay, bye," she said.

We talked throughout the night. The best night I have ever lived and dream to live again. In Engineers Palace everybody was asleep except for me.

"If your conversation is over, can you please switch off the lights, Mr. Devdas," said Sujeet ironically.

6

Proposal to Mingle

If a little dreaming is dangerous, the cure for it is not to dream less but to dream more; to dream all the time.

—Marcel Proust

The next day everybody went to college while I slept. I don't think I would have stopped sleeping till...

Tring, tring! "Tring, tring"! My telephone bell rang.

"Hello, who is there?"

"I could not go to college today all because of you," she complained.

She tried to stop her laugh.

"What did I do? Did I ask you not to go?"

"No," she said.

"There are plenty of red spots on my skin," she complained.

"Spots of mosquito bites."

"Yeah and it's looking so ugly." She complained that everybody was alleging that she had a boyfriend with whom she was talking till late at night.

"So, what can I do?" I asked.

"Let them talk," she answered. You know, these girls, they have a passive way of flirting with those they love.

Our talks continued for the next four hours. What is more, often our conversation was so long that many a times we had our breakfast at lunch time. She used to scintillate my mind and her talk used to sap my worries.

Days passed and we started regarding each other with respect and understand each other better. Once, I wanted to compliment her but could not gather enough courage. But, one day, I said, "The guy who marries you would be very lucky."

"Is it so? I don't think like that," she replied: "But one thing is sure—any girl would be desperate to get a husband like you."

I don't know why girls have the habit of giving back—you know, the barter system. If somebody were to invite us for dinner my mother would gear up to throw a small party promptly. Even a compliment has become a part of the barter system.

Those were the days when I had lost concentration in studies. Various assignments lay pending for days and months. I felt very happy when she was with me, be it in any form, and deeply sad when she was not there.

I would daydream in class and the one-hour lecture seemed to be one-year long; that means, four lectures seemed like four complete years.

At Engineers Palace my friends started ignoring me as I began avoiding them and the moments together. I was not in my senses; I was in another world. One day, not knowing what was there in Shikha's mind, I told her various things about my roommates.

"I don't like that guy (one of my friends)," she said.

"Why, what happened?" I enquired.

She said something. I don't remember right now, but, it was not a compliment.

"I cannot listen anything being said against my friends," I remarked sternly. I overreacted.

I don't know, whether it's a flaw to love my friends and people, and those who are very close to me.

When I divulged this to my friends, they said that it was not the right way to react.

Next day I found that Shikha was distressed and behaved as though I had maltreated her. I felt very sad. But how could she erase my words from her mind? "Agreed I was a bit blunt, but I never meant to hurt you," I tried to convince her.

"You are a maniac," she shot back.

"Thanks for the compliment. But, when did you discover that?" I asked.

These words irritated her all the more. "You are mad," she retorted.

"C'mon, Shikha. Don't behave like a kid."

There was no reply.

"I'm sorry," I pleaded.

Again no reply.

"I'm sorry," I repeated.

Again no reply.

"I'm sorry."

She giggled like anything; I had never seen Shikha laugh so hysterically. "You are mad and I like this madness," she said. "You are really very nice. But do not ever scold me. I could not sleep last night. When are you offering me a treat?"

"Very soon," I replied.

My friends pressed me to propose to her.

"What will people say? Pankaj, the talented one among us, could not propose to the girl he loved," said Amit. "You are at the zenith of love."

Whether love vibrates or resonates in people's lives or not, it is something which has survived and continues to exist. I passed that night restlessly with all kinds of thoughts assailing my mind. What should I do? Should I propose? Is it the right time? For the first time I was in a dilemma.

Next came the day I was desperately waiting for—'the proposal to mingle'.

I was back at Engineers Palace after finishing my classes. Seriously speaking, I did practice a number of times with each of my roommates how and what I would say, so as to weed out the shortcomings, if any.

The rehearsals continued for an hour or so, until a green signal was given. "It will be interesting to hear how this guy proposes," said Ritesh.

The dialogue which was prepared ran thus:

"Will you be my fiancé?"

But as usual, the fate of all first-time lovers is same. As they lack experience, they commit the mistake which they should not. While I was busy talking to her, I forgot my dialogue. Anyway, our conversation continued. We talked of everything except the proposal. Finally, after inhaling all the oxygen present in the air, I proposed to Shikha, "I would like to marry you, Will you marry me?" I asked.

I don't know how a blunt guy like me could speak those words so beautifully. My voice (at that time) could easily be compared to a nightingale's.

There was silence; pin-drop silence. I could hear my heart-beats which were pounding at tremendous pace till...

"It can't be better than to marry a person who loves me and I know him so well. To marry a person like you would be divine." (See the gravity of statement!) "But before coming to a decision, let me tell you something about my past—things which I have never discussed with you."

I have always been a clever person. I knew everything about her past and present, about the guys who were attached to her and also about the persons who were associated with her. Nevertheless, I thought, let her speak.

She told me about the guys who had proposed to her; they were many in number. She told me different stories altogether—

a different story for a different guy. I interrupted her many times, but she held me back from doing so. In her entire narrative, one single guy stood out. Let us remember his name... Yeah, got it! Vikas.

"Vikas proposed to me several times. He used to help me always, but I never regarded him more than a good friend. He used to send me several beautiful messages. At first I ignored them, but later I started replying..."

"So what? It happens in today's life, too," said an impatient Pankaj in me.

"Let me complete first," she said. "Now, Vikas proposed to me. I rejected his proposal, but he continued to help me in every way and I began liking him. Vikas and many of our friends, including I, used to party together and indulge in things which college students usually do."

Now, the word 'Vikas' began to trouble me. She was telling her love story to the guy who loved her the most (imagine the situation). But, I had no option but to listen.

"Everybody, I mean Vikas's friends, told me that he loved me immensely. So when he proposed me for the third time, I could not say 'no'. I accepted his proposal, but I never proposed to him. We started going together for movies and spend time in restaurants. This love continued for a few months until the chameleon changed its colour. This wicked guy ditched me, saying that our career was more important and love was not something to be continued forever. Love was not permanent and that he was interested in another girl called Neema.

"When I returned to the hostel, I cried uncontrollably. Everybody tried to make me understand, but it took me months to get over him. He, however, continued to message me but I never replied. I do not care for him and neither do I talk to him now."

"Anything else Ma'am?" I asked.

"No," she replied curtly.

"Do you think you are the only person in this entire world who has been ditched by someone?" I asked. "There are numerous such cases. I would rather say it has became a part of the life of the younger generation and these things are bound to happen. If we are surrounded by some good people, then we are bound to be surrounded by some bad people too."

I continued, "Why do you care for such guy who hardly cares for you? In one short sentence, it was not love. Was it?" I asked.

"Yes, you are right," she mumbled.

I tried to make her as comfortable as I could by cracking some jokes. I even added, "You know Shikha, I knew of all these things."

"Is it so? Who told you?" she queried.

"That hardly matters. What matters is that I love you, love you, love you."

She blushed.

It was a four-hour long conversation.

Everybody at Engineers Palace congratulated me for loving her not only with my heart but also with my spirit. She was like oxygen for me which is necessary for the sustenance of human life.

7

Dream Date

They are not long, the days of wines and roses; out of a misty dream our path emerges for a while, then closes within a dream.

—Ernest Christopher Dowson

I felt as though I was floating in air. What added to my overall euphoric feeling of triumph was the fact that she had accepted my proposal.

She used to seek the blessings of her *ishta devata* (family God) every day. She was a devout devotee who visited the temple, church, etc. She was pure in heart, with prejudice towards none. Life became normal for me. I felt like a settled person. Love blossomed in my heart and it reflected on my face. One day she visited the *mazar* in the evening. I wanted to accompany her but she said, "Only a married couples go together, step in step."

I must say, this added to my knowledge. "No, I will come with you," I persisted.

"Is this a festival?" she asked.

"Most definitely," I replied.

"That's ridiculous, Pankaj. Why don't you understand?" she begged.

"Okay, no issues. But next time I will accompany you and that's for sure," I replied.

"Fine," she said.

She was the one who decided the venue for our dates and the timings too. I decided on the date this time.

Then came the most precious time of my life—the day for our date. It was a Thursday. We (my friends and I) did shopping in the morning.

It was the first date of my life, so, it had to be the best. I dressed in the best, I could. I was so excited; in fact, the environment at Engineers Palace was as exciting as one could imagine. My eyes were on the wall-clock. I thought its arms moved rather slowly.

"One hour left," announced Anurag.

We had some dazzling snapshots to post on the Orkut.

It was like a procession. I kept all my credit cards and cash in my pockets as if a king was out on a date with his queen.

"I have reached here..." she said.

"Wait for five minutes and you'll find me."

"Okay," she replied.

When I reached the spot, she was looking extraordinarily beautiful in a black top with short sleeves and trousers which were grey. I simply say 'grey' because I lack the vocabulary to describe the colour of her trousers. Her hair was tied back with a clip which enhanced her beauty. It was a snazzy combination and she dazzled! She was flamboyant!

As the restaurant was some distance away, we walked together. It was a cosy restaurant, but if I had to select the restaurant, it would have been a multi-starred one.

We went upstairs. It was our first eye-to-eye contact. She had told me earlier that she did not talk much, but, it was my ability which tempted even the rocks to speak.

First we had hors d'oeuvre and then we ordered lunch. Of course, all the dishes were of her choice as I was busy looking at her. At first, she was reluctant to make eye contact with me for a long time as she blushed with shyness.

"How will you convince my father?"

This question of hers hit me like a bullet. I had no idea as to how I could convince her father. But, I had to give her a convincing answer. I tried to convince her and I think she was.

This also made me realise that she was her father's daughter and a family-oriented girl. This increased my love for her manifold.

"But how will you convince my mother?" she enquired further.

I let the subject drop, assuming that it was Shikha's usual flip repartee.

We talked about various things (the normal young-generation talk). She asked me about my future plans.

"What's your future plan?"

"To keep loving you," I replied.

"Apart from that?" she asked.

"I want to be a software engineer and later become the boss of some software firm."

Well, we had our cups and sat at peace with absolutely nothing to say to one another. So, I raised a topic. "You know, to be a part of these firms, you need to have a great analysing power," I began.

"That means Pankaj would also be a good observer."

"That's for sure, Ma'am," I said.

"If you don't mind, should I cross-check your discerning ability?" she queried,

I had to impress her, no matter how. I gave the whole situation a big think for about two seconds and reached a succinct conclusion, "Okay, go on."

"See that couple behind you and describe them—everything except their behaviour. You can look behind for a fraction of a second."

The situation depicted a scene from the *Mahabharata* when Arjun had to aim his arrow at the eyes of the revolving fish. He succeeded, but what about me? I looked behind for some nanoseconds and then turned to look into Shikha's eyes.

I began to describe—

"One boy and one girl, sitting opposite each other. The girl is wearing a *salwar* suit combination of sky blue and white. Her hair is open and on the table there are two cans of Pepsi and one sandwich. The boy is wearing a green coloured shirt with white stripes and black trousers. His style is simple and he has a round face and..."

She interrupted me, "Okay, impressed! You are a great observer!" she said.

It was late evening, when she said, "Should we leave now?"

As usual I said, "Okay, half-an hour more."

The restaurant was filled with couples and each pair of eyes seemed to spend its maximum time on us. To enjoy some lighter moments, I said, "Whenever couples go to a restaurant or anywhere else, girls seem interested in other guys except their boyfriend and boys are interested in girls other than their girlfriend."

"How true!" she laughed.

"And you are interested in..."

"Nobody," she laughed like anything.

Time passed and now we had to hurry.

At Engineers Palace, everybody was waiting for me to return. As soon as I entered, they celebrated with Cokes and sprayed it on me. All my clothes got drenched in the shower of Coke.

"What happened?" asked Sujeet.

"Did you impress her?" added Anurag.

"What did she say?" asked Amit.

"How did she react?" It was Ritesh's turn.

"One at a time, please," I begged. "Let me take a deep breath."

"You can do that afterwards," said Ritesh.

Everybody was desperate to know how the day had passed and I was the centre of attraction at Engineers Palace.

"Now, just tell us everything one by one..."

Ritesh interrupted Sujeet to say, "And step by step."

So, I told them, step by step. Many a times they interrupted me to give their generous opinions (free of cost).

"So, cool," they said in one voice.

"What did you expect? I love her *yaar*; I didn't have any amorous desires," I said.

Ritesh, the last guy to complete the family at Engineers Palace, was the most casual one. The word 'tension' was missing from his dictionary. He was a perpetual flirt. He had a vacillating nature and never stuck to one girlfriend for long as there was always another tied to his belly.

The grandeur at the Palace increased where we had some of our guests what we called 'palace-guests'. As a matter of fact, Engineers Palace had five permanent members but many temporary members. So, it can be said that Engineers Palace was a dwelling place for many. It was a place for everything except studies. Daily we would gear up for some celebration for some or the other.

We would pull each other's leg, crack jokes, play and chat with girls on internet—our favourite timepass. When talking to Shikha, somewhere from within, the moments used to energise me and fill me with renewed determination and confidence. I endeavoured to be genuinely concerned, sincere and compassionate.

8

Fun at Engineers Palace

*Those women who can see their lovers even in dreams are lucky,
but without him sleep won't come; so who can dream a dream?*

—Hla Stauhane

One day (let me remember), it was Tuesday, when something horrible happened which left us all at Engineers Palace terribly frightened.

We had a maid who did all the cooking. She remained away from work without prior information. So, we engineers substituted as chefs for the day. It was 10 o'clock at night when our cooking gas finished. So, we had to replace the cylinder with a new one which we had in our stock. When Sujeet replaced it, it leaked out slowly. For confirmation, he kindled a matchstick and rotated it round the knob which fitted the cylinder's bore into the regulator. Suddenly, the bore caught fire and the flames began to soar higher. He cried out, "Fire, fire."

From my room I rushed, quaking, trembling with fear. Soon we all rushed to the spot, but the flames rose seven feet in height. We began to scream in terror, our senses failing to work. It was a terrible situation. Two buckets of water were kept near the cylinder, but, as I said, our senses were not working. The fire started soaring till it touched the ceiling, which was about ten feet in height. Amit brought a bucket of water and poured it on the knob. It hardly made any difference. Then Ritesh poured two buckets of water kept beside the cylinder. We could not bear the intense heat. Sujeet stood rooted to the spot. After having poured about twenty-five buckets of water, the fire showed some kindness: the flames began to decrease. After much effort, the fire was brought under control.

With our hearts thudding, we heaved a sigh of relief. We had a close shave with death. Soon we all began to laugh, out of relief after such a tense situation.

"Just see the situation! Sujeet knew that there was leakage because of the lousy smell that was being emitted, but he kindled the matchstick," complained Ritesh.

"It just happened. I don't know how, but it happened," murmured Sujeet.

"Okay, no issues; whatever has happened has happened. Three cheers for our resurrection," said Anurag.

Next day we shared this episode with our other friends in college with some spices added, to make it sound more horrible.

"Oh! how terrifying it was!" commented one of our friends.

I concluded that our senses have very limited power. There are many defects in our conditioned state. However 'when helpers fail and comforts are free', there is always someone to lend a helping hand.

Next morning, I didn't even wave to her or even look her way, and yet she thought I was watching her.

I dialled her number in the evening.

"I am out with my roommate. I am here in a temple," she said.

"Okay, that means you are praying for my well-being," I said.

"Yes and various others, like my parents," she added. "I have to offer some flowers, so can we talk after some time?"

"Okay. Actually I wanted to share a terrifying experience, which happened last night. Anyway, I will call you later," I added.

"Tell me right now. Is everything okay?" she enquired.

"I am absolutely fine and I will call you at night. I have to visit my friend's place now," I said.

You know these girls—they cannot live with half information. They need all the details and this is what I like in girls. One more thing which impresses me in girls is their endurance power. What I had loved about Shikha was her ability to penetrate her glance inside me to understand things I could never carve out in words.

She called me at night. "Now, tell me what happened yesterday," she said, matching her own generosity of spirit.

I told her everything. Even she became terrified as I am quite an eloquent person when describing the gory details.

"Can't you take care of yourself and this is what you do in your Engineers Palace?" she complained in a way that made me laugh. "Should I suggest something? Why don't you marry someone?"

Girls have a passive way of flirting with guys they love.

"Don't give me that 'someone' crap," I said bluntly. "I will marry 'you'." I said that as ominously as I could, sort of implying that I would punch out any rival who would creep within my sight.

"How long will you love me. Will you love me if I do not talk to you properly?"

Hear what I had to say—"A saint was rescuing a scorpion that had fallen into a pond. Every time he lifted it out of water, it stung him but he would not give up until it was saved. One of his disciples asked why he was persistent in saving the scorpion that stung him. The *sadhu* replied: 'The nature of a scorpion is to sting; the nature of a saint is to rescue a being in distress. So long as the scorpion does not give up its work, why should I give up mine?'

"The nature of the fire is to burn, of water is to cool, of wind is to blow and of Pankaj is to love Shikha."

"You are the ultimate; you are invincible," she conceded.

In our conversation later, she mentioned once that she would stagnate if I left her at any stage. So, I took a vow, from that day onward to love and cherish Shikha, till death do us apart.

To know her more closely, I approached Shreya, our common friend. "Hey Shreya, I want to ask you something about..." I began.

"About whom?" she queried.

"Shikha," I replied.

"But you know her better. She talks to you...and I don't know much about her," she added. I did everything to please her, every damn possible thing, but she seemed reluctant. I feel irritated when you talk about Shikha," she said.

I don't know what pleased Shreya, but she was unbearable. She used to repulse me whenever I asked for her help in this matter. 'Was she in nemesis?' I thought several times. All sorts of questions about her used to haunt me. I tried to convince her that she was a friend, philosopher and guide of Shikha.

Constant hope makes our life liveable. It's up to us to treat life as a problem or opportunity.

Our love went on waxing and we continued to share our feelings, our desires, every day. It (talking) was now a morning, evening and night affair. According to her, every event meant a purpose and every setback its lesson.

Once, during our conversation, she asked me casually, "Do you believe in multiple affairs?"

"No, I don't."

"I hate those people who are engaged in multiple affairs," she said.

"What about extra-marital affairs?" I said playfully.

"Marital," Shikha pointed out politely, since I had mispronounced it for the first and only time in my Goddamn life.

After hearing this, I felt great exultation.

"This is definitely one of the memorable moments of my life," she remarked.

"What's memorable in it?"

"Today, I was your mentor."

We both started to laugh, softly at first. Soon our giggles turned into guffaws. Shikha certainly never lost her sense of humour that kept me entertained for so long.

"What is your favourite time-pass?" I asked.

"I'll tell you, but first promise you will not laugh," she begged.

"Okay," I said.

"Sleeping."

"Do you know why people sleep so much?" I asked.

"Why?"

"Because they really don't have anything else to do," I replied.

"No, I do a lot of things and sleep only in my spare time," she said.

"Most people live at such a frenetic pace that they cannot find comfort in silence. They don't have the time to build friendships or spend some time with their friends, if they have any," I said.

"How true! But how do you know such people?"

"Because I was one of them," I said.

I observed a sense of joy in my life along with the ability to appreciate things that surrounded me. Each day, no matter how busy I was or how many challenges I faced, I never bowed down to the circumstances.

9

Ishita, the Love Guru

A lady's imagination is very rapid; it jumps from admiration to love, from love to matrimony in a moment.

—Jane Austen

I was in Standard XII, when we had a guest (I don't remember his name) from the USA. He was a great motivator. About three hundred students were seated in the school auditorium, surrounded by school teachers.

He asked, "Where do you find yourself after ten years from now?"

Many of us raised our hands to answer his question. All of us had almost the same answer. "We will be working in a good firm, that is, a good job."

"Okay."

"Where do you find yourself after twenty years from now?" he asked.

"I see myself well settled as a General Manager of a reputed firm," I said.

Almost all of us had the same answer as our intellectual power was almost the same.

"Okay. Now the last question. Where do you find yourself after forty years from now?"

None of us could visualise to that extent. But one of us answered, "I see myself as the president of a multinational firm."

"I had not expected a better answer. You are simply ordinary. But the world today needs extraordinary people," the motivator replied. "The world is moving at a rapid pace. We must be geared up for that."

"If everybody would search for a job, who would be there to employ them? Our knowledge of any subject cannot be perfected unless we receive it through authoritative sources. If we have the habit of comparing ourselves with others, our self-confidence sometimes soars and sometimes crashes. A truly extraordinary life is never based on comparison. It is the result of constant *ishita*—the love-*guru* blossoming within.

"If every circumstance is to our liking, the internal growth and transformation will never take place. Our life will became stagnant and sub-human."

"Be an entrepreneur and flow like a river, revelling in every moment of life."

Those magical words—'be an entrepreneur'—changed the way I had so far lived my life. I began to follow the principle of 'go big or stay home' from that day onwards.

To let this happen, I needed to be strategic, conversant, optimistic, analytical and diligent. I developed all these qualities in me and today I am geared up to be an entrepreneur.

We had our classes daily from 10 a.m. to 4 p.m. On Saturdays, it used to be a different ball game. We had our personality development classes, where everybody learnt to groom themselves in their snazzy-cosy clothes.

I had a number of friends with whom I used to spend most of the time in college. I used to notice her and so did she. I don't know whether she wanted to spring a real surprise upon me.

We would pass by and smile to each other, feeling entirely satisfied with the others. Our love in college was speechless, soundless; it was a silent love. She always hesitated when passing me, no matter where I was.

"Why do you hesitate so much?" I asked her once.

"I feel shy," she admitted.

Whether it was the marvel of the starry night or the scorching sun of daytime, we both were ever-anxious. Sometimes we used to discuss points of philosophy and enjoy the pleasures of each other's company. We felt as if we were on Shikaj—the Shikha and Pankaj name of the 13th planet (imaginary). Citizens of this palace looked youthful and moved with poise and purpose. Love had elevated the quality of my life and replenished my sense of wonder at the world we lived in. My friends however had a different view. "You are becoming more joyful and spontaneous; growing more energetic but lacking creativity, for which you are known. You do not even perform well nowadays," said Ritesh.

Though the conviction with which he spoke was clear, I began to grow sceptical. Was I a victim of some prank? After all, Ritesh was known for his practical jokes.

"When Shikha comes here, she would be an honorary member and integral part of our extended family in Engineers Palace," suggested Amit.

We used to foresee the future in European chateaus and admire it as altruistic and whose power was buttressed by love.

One day, I received a call from Ishita, my childhood friend. She had rung me after six months.

"Hey Pankaj, it's me, Ishita. How are you?" she asked.

"I'm fine, Ishita. Where have you been all these days and what were you doing?" I asked curiously.

"Just enjoying the fantasies around; you know my style of living," she stated. "How are your studies going on?" she asked.

"Very slow."

"Why?"

"Because I am in love," I shot back.

"How could this be possible? I mean, a person like you in love and what about your ego? Is it intact?"

"She has never hurt my ego."

"May I know the name of that magician?"

"Shikha," I blurted out.

"Okay Pankaj, I got to go now. I'll definitely ring you tomorrow."

Ishita, my childhood friend, was a naughty, playful and charming girl. We used to study in the same school. She was my classmate up to Standard XII, when she went away to Pune to pursue her higher education. She was the most flirtatious girl in the school. Ishita had never been a good student but was a bright teacher, friend, philosopher and guide in the true sense and that is why she was popularly known as Ishita, the love guru. Everybody (teachers excluded, even though some young teachers did) in school shared their difficulties with her and she used to offer an ultimate solution. During my schooling, I was least interested in anything except studies. Many girls including Ishita tried their luck on this hardcore rock, but their attempts failed every time. They called me a blunt and egoistic guy. But, we were friends and helped each other under every circumstance. But, this time it was a big deal!

Shikha was very happy as if she was flying high up in the sky. She had no big desires, no big dreams, but she had sweet dreams and it was certain that in the coming (near) future, I would have made her dreams a reality.

We (my friends and I) were watching a horror movie, in which a crumpet woman, who used to be normal during daytime, would become a ghost every night to cause numerous deaths. Suddenly my telephone bell rang.

It was Shikha. "Hey, what were you doing?" she asked.

"I was talking to Ishita, my girlfriend."

"Then I must have disturbed you. I'll talk to you later," she retorted.

"Hey, I was watching a movie."

"I knew it," she said.

"What?" I asked.

"You cannot have another girlfriend."

"Why, am I not smart?" I asked.

"You are smart. But you are not smart in flirting with girls," she clarified.

"You are very smart in flirting with boys," I prompted.

"Thank you so much," she said. We laughed and laughed until our stomachs began to pain.

"Shikha, do you believe in necromancy and black magic?" I asked.

"No, I do not believe in those things. I believe in God, but I have heard about them from some of my friends," she replied.

"My friends say that I don't have time to improve upon my thoughts and that my life has become stagnant," I said.

"Because you spend so much time talking to me," she remarked.

"Maybe," I replied.

"I too feel that you need to pay attention to your goal. After all, you plan to be an entrepreneur," she said.

"They tease me, saying that once our conversation gets cracking, I don't find even ten minutes to have lunch," I said.

"Is it so? Tell me frankly," she said.

"Sometimes," I remarked.

"So, from now on, be regular in your diet, else I'll not talk to you," she gave the ultimatum.

"Okay, no issues. I'll be regular," I said.

She once asked me, "Will I be a good entrepreneur?"

"Why not use what talent you possess? The woods would be very silent if no birds sang except those that sing the best.

You have to learn how to present yourself and everything else will be fine."

My friends complained that I did not spend much time with them. I used to be a regular absentee in palace affairs. It was incredible to admit this but it was a fact. Many a times I thought of making them understand, but I was lost in my own passion.

After two days, Ishita rang me. "You are calling me now," I complained.

"I am so sorry, I got stuck with some work."

"You don't need to be that sorry; it's fine," I said.

"Okay, how is she doing?" she asked.

"Shikha is fine."

"Did you propose to her?"

"Yes, I did."

"What was her reaction?"

"She showed a mixed reaction, but it was laced with optimism."

"Then, you must be rocking."

"Yeah, I am."

"What are your plans ahead?"

"To marry her after completing my studies."

"I am dying to talk to her. Should I talk to her?"

"No," I stopped her.

"Why?" she asked with a kind of disdain.

"I'll let you talk at an appropriate time," I remarked.

"Okay, I just wanted to chat with that lucky girl who could find a place in the heart of this 'hardcore rock'. What do you like in her?" she asked.

"Everything," I said.

"Everything means?"

"I like her as a person—her simplicity, endurance, her activities, her nature, her voice, face...everything."

"What do you dislike in her?" she asked.

"There is nothing that I dislike. But, there are things which I do not praise. After all, she is a human being."

10

Pankaj, Half Dead

Every age yearns for a more beautiful world. The deeper the desperation and the depression about the confusing present, the more intense that yearning.

—Johan Huizinga

Just visualise my passion—I used to talk to her even when the electricity went off and I sweated out in the heat.

My punch line was—'If everything seems to be in control, you are not moving fast enough.'

This had always helped me in the worst of circumstances, but by engaging in subtle labelling, I tried to create something in the current realities every moment.

Everything went on smoothly. I was a cool man who used to revel in all I experienced. One day Shikha revealed, "You know Pankaj, I always fear what would happen if our relationship was not to continue."

"Why do you feel like that?" I asked. "Don't you trust me?"

"I trust you, but I do not trust my fate," she had said.

I just sat there with a 'no-expression' look on my face,

"Don't worry, everything will be alright. I will not let anything enter into our relationship," I assured her.

A profound understanding between us nullified all the worries. But, I could not sleep that night. I kept thinking about Shikha's words. I could never imagine life without her.

I scanned around and found only 'Ishita, the love guru' to come to my help. So, I rang her at 2 o'clock at night. Ishita was fast asleep. I rang her twice before she received the call.

"Calling a girl at 2 o'clock at night? Am I in danger (what a *flirt*)? Is your intension pious?"

"Just shut-up," I said in a disdain manner.

"Okay, what happened?"

I told her what was bothering me.

"She might have tossed a bone."

"No, she was serious," I said.

"Just give her some more time. Let her relax and try to mull over the matter which is holding her back. Be patient. Don't get annoyed or irritated. I know you, but you need to keep your cool," she said.

"But..."

"Do you remember our physics teacher telling us that Einstein once said, *"Everything happening in this world is a miracle, or nothing happening in this world is a miracle."* We need to believe any one of these to escape the saturnine life. Just believe in yourself. I know things will be fine."

"Ishita, you are simply the best," I said.

"Ishita knows that," she said gaily.

Next day, our landlord invited us to the marriage of her grand-daughter. Engineers Palace was decorated with all sorts of lights; it looked marvellous. It was again party time for the engineers of Engineers Palace.

You know, these marriage parties tempt you to think about your dream girl and give you so much pain that it hurts when she is not there. And my friends were interested in every other girl. Anyway, we enjoyed immensely and danced so enthusiastically as if it was our friend's marriage. I felt satisfied with my relationship with Shikha. In fact, sometimes I felt as if she was there. I had read somewhere that true love is selfless and that such love brings about lasting peace and happiness. I realised it was true.

Shikha was a good painter and great singer—both were her hobbies. She was a fan of Atif Aslam, the singer. She sang beautifully and had a melodious voice.

Once I asked her to sing a song. And you know what? She sang. Her song reminded me of the nightingale and frog.

"And, of course, I wield my pen
for Bog trumpet now and then."
"Did you.... did you like my song?"
"Not too bad but far too long.
The technique was fine, of course,
but it lacked a certain force."
"Oh!" the nightingale confessed.
Greatly flattered and impressed
that a critic of such note
had discussed her art and throat:
"I don't think the song's divine,
but, oh! Well, at least its mine."

I clapped because it was so nice and soothing while I was a mere bathroom singer. Then came a revelation—I discovered what made her hold back every now and then.

"There is a proposal for my marriage," she said.

"I know, I only proposed to you," I said casually.

"Other than you," she said.

"Means the entry of a villain," I laughed.

"They are coming to see me."

"When?"

"This Sunday. My parents will arrive by Saturday."

"Where does the guy live?"

"Chennai."

"What does he do?"

"He runs a family business and invests in shares. They are very rich," she said.

"Are you interested in him?" I asked.

"Yes, I am very much interested," she retorted sarcastically.

"Okay, then..."

"Hey, wait a sec."

"What happened?" she asked

"Nothing," I said.

"Don't badger, Pankaj. Tell me, why would he marry me? He is rich and prefers a business lady who can help him but I have no M.B.A. degree even."

"Okay, whatever be the condition, just say 'no' to them."

"As you wish, but don't be tense," she said.

Then, started my saturnine days. My friends were very good, but they could not understand my condition. I tried my best to be normal. I used to think that Sunday would be a 'dark day' for me but my subconscious told me that it would be a 'bright day'.

It felt good to talk to Shikha; without that, I passed horrendous moments.

As the day approached near, I spent sleepless nights as if my life had gone. I could not pay attention to my studies; everything for me was vague, life looked fragile. I couldn't tell what pleased me. I was frazzled. Every night I hoped for a fragrant morning, 'but what about Sunday' came to question my jumping mind.

My mother rang me to enquire about my well-being.

"How are you, son?" she asked.

"I am fine," I said.

"I had a nightmare last night. I saw you feeling very sad," she said.

"No, I am very happy; the happiest guy."

"You are very careless. Please take care of yourself."

"Don't worry. I will do that."

"Is something troubling you?"

"No."

"You are sounding depressed."

"No, nothing of that sort."

"I will visit you next Sunday."

"My exams are approaching. I need to study."

"Don't take extra pressure and be happy. I am greatly concerned for you."

"Just relax, I am fine," I said.

Talking to my mother gave me no relief. On the contrary, the dam of emotions burst open. In those days I used to call Shikha at regular intervals. It was Saturday when...

"Hey Shikha, have your parents arrived?" I asked

"They will be here in two hours' time."

"Okay."

"Pankaj, are you alright?"

"Yeah."

"Sure?" she asked.

"Yeah, sure."

"Why do you think so much?"

" I said, I'm fine."

"I also don't want to marry that guy. I don't know him. Because of my parents, I need to go there and I can't say 'no' to my parents. Nothing is decided. Okay?"

"Yeah, okay."

Even Shikha sounded dejected.

I liked Shikha's parents in every way except one. Shikha had imbibed really good moral and behaviour from her parents, but not their thinking, which was orthodox. Shikha was untouched by their thinking, though regarding the question of marriage, her parents' opinion mattered the most. She told me that once her family was invited to attend a reception. It was a love-cum-arranged marriage. A friend of Shikha's mother asked her, "Would you allow your daughter to marry a person of her choice, if all other conditions are fulfilled?"

"My girl will marry the boy of my choice," her mother had said.

Mothers are very good to their children. They want them to be happy, but some do not have progressive thinking. Their imagination is limited and they can't look beyond...

It was the day; it was *the* Sunday.

Since it was a holiday, the day passed in chatting with friends who visited us. New stories about different experiences kept me busy. However, I kept my fingers crossed throughout the day.

Shikha called me in the evening.

"What happened. Did you say no?" I asked desperately.

"No," she said.

"I mean what? Yes or no?" I asked.

"My father said 'no'. I could not get my turn to speak," she said.

"Why?"

"Actually, their demands were very high. More than what we can afford," she said.

"Were you interested in him?"

"No way. I was not," she said. "Now, are you happy?"

"I am in ecstasy," I replied.

Suddenly, I felt very happy and relieved. I had been listening to soothing music all these days but now I turned to rock music. I hoped for some leisurely days ahead.

Life started flowing like a gentle breeze. I used to get enthralled by observing and experiencing the wonder and beauty in every single thing around me. All the threads of my dream were woven around Shikha. Everything moved smoothly from thereon—similar routine, similar schedule, same affair.

One day my brother called me and we planned a trip to Shimla with some of his friends. I knew most of his friends, so much so that some of his friends were even my close friends.

Meantime I had a talk with Ishita, the love guru.

"How is your love-life going?" she asked.

"It could have taken a U-turn, but everything is fine with God's grace," I answered.

"What happened?" she asked.

I told her the events of the past week which had disturbed me.

"It's ludicrous. Why didn't she tell everything clearly to her parents?"

"They are orthodox."

"So what? They are still her parents. They will listen to her," she said.

"I am still studying, Ishita," I said.

"The matter is becoming serious. Are you attached to her mentally?" she asked.

"Spiritually," I replied.

"Oh God! I had never imagined that a person like you..." she stopped.

"Anyway, what are her plans ahead?" she asked.

"She does not have clear-cut plans," I said.

"Just pursue that conjuror to do a job. Ask her to be career-oriented and even she wants that, as you had said earlier. I know you can do that," she said.

"Okay!"

"In fact, provide her a job. You have a number of contacts; use those. I know you can do it."

"That's a pretty easy task for me. But, will she accept that?" I said doubtfully.

"Why are you thinking so much? Just relax. Pursue her, not to get immersed in those damn marriage proposals all the time. There are other aspects of life too," she said.

I consistently framed my experiences that empowered me and made my life more workable and enjoyable. Perhaps Shikha's fascination for me stemmed from my deep feelings and emotions which were linked to my process of thinking and thoughts. Our mind and intellect combined to generate strong likes and dislikes, leading us to love each other immensely. We were enjoying and lost in our dreams.

Once Shikha described a sweet dream that she had seen. "I saw Brad Pitt proposing to me, yesterday," she said.

"What did you reply?" I asked.

"'Yes', obviously 'yes'," she said.

"That's great," I said.

"When is he visiting you again for the ring ceremony?" I asked.

These girls, they always try to pull your leg and make you feel small. This might be true, but she was telling this to her lover. Why, so?

"He was sartorially subtle," she added further.

"Then, go and marry him," I suggested. "Or, isn't it fun enough?"

"You know Pankaj, I feel you will take revenge for all the naughty things I do when we are married," said Shikha demurely and ingenuously.

"No, in fact I will enjoy that. You have a true lively nature," I said.

"Hey, I did not know," she said.

"Then, know about it now," I retorted. "I do not sleep properly nowadays."

"And neither do you let me sleep," she added.

"Is it so?" I asked.

"Just wait a minute. There is another call," she said.

"Cancel it," I pleaded.

"No, I need to attend to it. He is a good friend of mine."

"Okay."

I used to get disgruntled by the numerous delays, but one has to cope with these things when one is in love. These things need tolerance which I didn't possess, but somehow I could manage. She was back on the line.

"I hope, I didn't keep you waiting."

"Actually, you did," I replied.

"That means you didn't disconnect," she said.

"That's a logical conclusion," I said, unable to sustain this kind of banter.

Shikha was indefatigable. She was the ultimate. "It's late at night and I am yawning."

"Then?" I said.

"Should I sleep?" she asked.

"And before that?"

"Good night, sweet dreams."

I could never go to sleep without saying this. Her wishes were as vital as vitamins for me which made me strong to start the next day. Those days, I used to keep a very tight schedule as I needed to spare a big chunk of my time for Shikha—my love, my life.

Ishita always told me to have patience, but I was impatient. "You need to concentrate less on your love life. Go easy. Don't take extra pains; do not remain in extreme states—either you are frazzled or in ecstasy. Just try to maintain a balance and don't panic," Ishita advised.

11

Fight with Fate

If the wind will not serve, take to the oars.

—Latin proverb

The next three days were holidays. Shikha had to visit her friend's home. My brother asked me to reach station on time to catch the train for Shimla. I had changed my mind as I needed blessings from God. I decided to persuade my brother to take me for a three-day trip to Agra, Mathura and Vrindavan.

At first he seemed reluctant, but I convinced him. After all he was my loving brother. May God give a brother like him to everybody. His type is badly needed in this world.

Just imagine 'Agra, the city of love' and 'Mathura, the city of God of love'! Doesn't it make a good combination; at least it sounds good.

So I, with my brother and his friends, started on a three-day trip. Our journey was quite good but we saw people fight for seats even in reserved compartments.

When we reached Mathura, we hired a cab to tour the famous temples. We visited many temples of Mathura and in each temple I prayed to God to help 'Pankaj, the destitute guy', every time I folded my hands. The city of Mathura is a holy city. We ran into a large number of saints and the people were friendly and helpful. Every single moment, two things were uppermost in my mind—Shikha and Shri Krishna.

After visiting the temples of Mathura, we started on our journey to Vrindavan. We hired a guide who told us the history of the places we visited. As we travelled along the outskirts of Vrindavan, we stopped to see the Kunj forest which spread over a large area. "Here Lord Shri Krishna used to play the flute to attract his lovers," said the guide.

The environment in Vrindavan was tranquil and filled with an aura of love.

It was very hot in the afternoon. The mercury was still rising and it had no intention to give up. As we went further, we came across an ancient temple which was quite dilapidated. But it attracted my attention for it was a marvellous piece of architecture. The sculptures were beautiful.

"If you circumambulate this temple, your desires are bound to be fulfilled," said the guide.

"Is it so?" I asked.

"It's nonsense," someone said.

The guide told me certain things which made me believe his statement. As I could not find anyone to come along with me, I decided to take a round of the temple by myself. As I placed my first step inside the temple, the soles of my feet burned as it was scorching hot. I saw some saints sitting in the shade.

As I stepped forward, my feet started burning severely. I could not take a step more, but I had to do it to ensure that Shikha would become a part of my fate. The soles which were used to the comfort of brands like Woodland and Red Chief were burning because of the boisterous sun. My state was miserable as I went further, but Shikha and Shri Krishna prodded me on. My body started boiling and I sweated profusely. My skin became red. I could not walk fast but I could not offered to be slow. My soles got red marks and the feet swelled. It took me one hour to complete one lap around the temple. I was very tired, yet we visited some more religious places.

I encountered a lot of problems while walking, but the thought of Shikha made me forget pain. After Vrindavan, we went to Agra. Since it was late in the evening, we went to a motel to stay. Agra, the city of love, is a beautiful place. At night, my soles were paining severely, so I was forced to swallow a pain-killer, but it hardly had any effect. Anyway, next morning I tried dialling Shikha's number.

"This number is either switched off or out of coverage area," the IVRS said.

Shikha had told me earlier not to talk for long when she was at her friend's house.

We went to see the Taj Mahal, the monument of love and one of the seven wonders of the world. The Taj Mahal was amazing! It was really beautiful! This was my first trip to Agra and the marvellous artifacts in marble were amazing! Foreigners also caught my attention. I never missed a chance to talk to them and take their snaps. We visited some more monuments of Agra and returned to the hotel. We had our lunch in a renowned restaurant of Agra. I found Agra beautiful and the people even more beautiful. We did some shopping.

I wanted to buy something for Shikha but I could not decide what to purchase as her number was out of reach. I dialled Ishita's number, but even her number was out of reach. I had no option but to drop the idea of buying something for her. The next day we had to return, but I wanted to visit to Fatehpur Sikri.

Fatehpur Sikri is a place of historic beauty, with a number of monuments. We visited some places including Saint Chishti's *mazar*. "If you tie a thread to the walls of the monument, your wishes are bound to be fulfilled," said one of the residents.

I did the same and wished what I desired. After visiting Fatehpur Sikri, we planned to return to our rooms as my soles pained unbearably.

While we were returning, I came across a girl, who was extremely beautiful. We were travelling on the same bus. Her hair were left free and her skin seemed flawless. We became very good friends in no time. She had a female companion with her.

"Is she your mother?" I asked.

"She is my sister," she said.

"Oh, I am so sorry."

"It's okay."

As we discussed, or rather I discussed, I told her about Shikha and my love for her.

"Shikha is very lucky," she remarked.

"Why?" I asked.

"Because you love her immensely and she knows it," she said. "There are very few people in this world who love their girlfriend to the extent you seem to do."

"She is not my girlfriend; she is my would-be wife," I intervened.

"That's very nice. Congratulations," she said.

Our conversation continued till my brother said ironically, "We have reached our destination. Shall we leave the bus now?"

"Oh, sure," I said. I bade her adieu.

It was 10 o'clock at night when I reached Engineers Palace. I received a warm welcome from my dear friends. I had lost a lot of water from my body because of sweat and thus felt exhausted.

As I took off my shoes, I saw my wounds bleeding. I was down with sunstroke.

"What is this? Did you hurt yourself there?" asked Anurag.

I told him about the visit.

"You are mad," he remarked.

"We know you love her, but why put yourself to pain?" asked Amit.

"If it was my case, I would have never done that. There is always another girl," said Ritesh.

After some time, I started belching, then vomitted a number of times. I collapsed and was rushed to the hospital. The doctor who examined me advised me to get admitted, but I refused. First he bandaged my soles and then inserted two injections into the veins of my arms.

"Drink a lot of water and glucose. You show symptoms of dehydration and sunstroke," said the doctor. Then he gave me the medical prescription listing medicines to be taken for the next 10 days.

Anyway, I felt fit and fine.

"What is this Pankaj? If this is love, I wish you had never fallen in love," said Sujeet.

"I will tell all this to Shikha. She only can cure you better," said Anurag.

"For God's sake, don't tell her," I screamed.

Suddenly, his mobile rang. It was Shikha's call. "Hi Anurag, how are you?" asked Shikha.

"We are in the hospital," said Anurag.

"What happened?" asked Shikha.

"Pankaj is ill. I'll talk to you later," said Anurag.

I thanked Anurag. I was fine, but my legs pained. I could not even place them on the ground properly. The doctor had advised me to take rest for at least five to six days.

'If Shikha will not find me in college, she would get very upset', I said to myself. So I decided to go to college the next morning.

"Are you going to college?" asked Amit.

"Yes," I replied.

"You are impossible," he said in anger.

I was in real trouble. My feet pained severely, but I survived.

I enjoyed every moment of my life. It was always full of wonder and never dull. Shikha rang me in the evening.

"Are you fine?" she asked in a worried tone.

"What can happen to me? I am pretty alright," I said.

"Just take care of yourself," she said.

"Okay, listen to me," I continued.

I told her everything about our tour, except...

"I rang you up several times from Agra," I said.

"Were you in trouble?" she laughed.

"Yeah, in real trouble."

"And, what was that?" she asked.

"I could not decide what to buy for you," I said. "I wanted to present you a small Taj Mahal. It was so nice."

She said that generally people do not present the Taj Mahal as it was built in the memory of one's love after her death.

Once again my knowledge waxed. The *Bhagvad Gita* says the world is 'the abode of sorrow' and 'a wild and terrible forest,' but for me the world was full of love—abundance of love.·

Love was the gift of life to me, without which I could not enjoy all that I had received.

Our thoughts were no longer limited to the present, but were now looking forward to the future.

One day, while I was talking to her, I asked, "Shikha, do you love me?"

"Hmmm," she said.

"Do you love me?" I repeated.

"No," she laughed.

"Do you love me?" I asked.

"What is this? Don't you know that?" she asked. "Yes, I love you. Shikha loves Pankaj," she added.

"What about our marriage?" I asked.

"If it's in our fate, nobody can separate us. We will surely get married," she said.

"Don't give me this moonshine talk," I said bluntly. "If this is your approach, we are bound to fail."

"Don't misconstrue," she quickly added. "Things will be fine."

12

Saturnine Days

Although it's difficult today to see beyond the sorrow; may looking back in memory help comfort you tomorrow.

—Author

After this started a series of numerous delays. She would say, "Our exams are approaching. We should stop our talks now."

"Okay, but we can at least talk for half an hour every day," I said.

"But, there are others also. If I provide each of them half an hour, when will I study?" she said.

"Okay, then I will not talk to you any more. If you feel like, you can talk to me," I said grudgingly.

"Okay," she said.

Then started my saturnine days. Suddenly life became boring and dull. I lost pleasure in work. All my friends in Engineers Palace knew this.

"Should I help you?" asked Anurag.

"No, it's not needed," I said.

Once Anurag met Shikha and he told her, "You do not call me nowadays. I want to discuss some matter with you," he added.

"I know that, but I need to hurry. We will talk later," she said.

Meanwhile, I rang Ishita.

"How is Shikha?" she asked.

"It's all over," I said.

"Elaborate."

"I have stopped talking to her," I said.

"Why? What happened?" she asked.

I told her everything.

"Don't you love her?" she asked.

"I love her immensely. She is my inspiration, my motivation; my everything," I cried.

"Don't stop. Just continue talking to her. Don't be depressed; go easy," she suggested.

By stripping things back to reality, we allow ourselves the freedom in each moment to consciously choose how to act and react. But I was depressed. My friends tried to help me out in every possible way, but I was preoccupied with memories of her.

I rang up Shikha after six days. "Hi, Shikha, how are you?" I asked.

"I am fine," she said. "Everything is over."

"Everything is intact," I persisted.

"When you do not call me, what do I presume? I will meet you for the last time after the exams," she said.

"Stop that lousy crap," I growled. "Within six days I have become mentally insane. I cannot live without you. Do not desert me," I pleaded.

"Because of you, my friends have stopped talking to me," she complained.

"Is it so?" I asked.

"Anurag used to talk to me regularly, but now he does not talk to me," she said.

"Okay, no issues. You will get a call from Anurag today itself," I said.

I pleaded with Anurag to talk to Shikha. At first he was reluctant, but later he nodded in approval.

These lines by poet Shelley aptly describe my life of those days.

> *Make me thylyre, even as the forest is:*
> *what if my leaves are falling like its own?*
> *The tumult of thy mighty harmonies,*
> *will take from both a deep autumnal tone,*
> *sweet though in sadness. Be thou, spirit fierce.*
> *My spirit! Be thou me, impetuous one!*

In the evening Anurag rang Shikha. "Hi Shikha, what's up?" he asked.

"I am fine," she answered. "And you?"

"On top of the world," he remarked.

"Why don't you talk to me nowadays?" she asked.

"I want to ask you something?" he said.

"Regarding Pankaj?" she volleyed back.

"Yes, since the last few days he has been upset and lost," he said. "Do you talk to him regularly?"

"Usually, we talk to each other," she said.

"Do you love Pankaj?" he asked.

"No, I don't. He always forced me to talk and I am not his colleague," she replied vehemently.

"Does that matter in love?" he asked.

"No, it doesn't," she said.

"Then, why did you start talking to him so much?" he asked.

"It was my childish behaviour," she admitted.

"Your childish behaviour has ruined somebody's life. Pankaj loves you immensely. And now, he is down with depression," he said.

"Why don't you make him understand?" she asked.

"Okay, I'll see to it. But don't stop talking to him," pleaded Anurag.

"Our exams are approaching and I can't talk to him much," she said.

"The most intelligent guy at Engineers Palace is in dumps now," he said.

"That's not my fault," she retorted.

She had one major flaw—her vacillating nature. She could be compared to a rotating coin which topples in any direction. She was pique and caprice.

I dialled her number several times but she never attended to my calls. I used to dial her phone number for hours continuously, but there was no response. Worry caused my mental and potential energy to wane. Suddenly all my creativity, optimism and motivation drained, leaving me exhausted. The mind can hold one thought at a time, and it was always the thought of Shikha. I always thought, 'She should not be, how can she be?'

I was deeply shattered. I turned to God to empathise with me. I asked, 'Why me?' There was no answer.

My semester exams began, but I had no interest. I could not study; I was completely lost. I was depressed.

In the meantime, she received my call. "Why don't you answer my call?" I asked.

She made a sarcastic remark which proved the *coup de grace*.

"You cannot distance yourself from me like this?" I said.

"I hate you," she said and disconnected the call.

This made me realise no matter how sure we are, we can never know each other thoroughly well.

I sent several voice messages, text messages, but there was no response. One day I received the news that she was down with fever. I rang her from a different number.

"How are you?" I asked.

"I am fine," she replied.

"And fever?" "Have you taken any medicine?" I asked.

"No, I rang my uncle for a prescription," she said. Then instantly she turned apologetically to me, "I am sorry for yesterday's conversation. I was a bit blunt. I don't want your life to be ruined. Just forget me," she said.

"My life is nothing without you," I said. "Okay, take care of yourself."

I left the following text message for her:

"My heart is in disarray,
my mind is reeling with distraction.
Each moment, every bit of me
keeps saying that
I miss you."

Subsequently she never received my call. Even in the examination hall, I would think about Shikha. She had deserted me but not my mind.

She once rang up Anurag and asked, "What should I do?"

"You should know that better," he said.

"I had consulted some of my friends but they didn't praise him and even called him rowdy," she said.

"I know that Pankaj is the best boy around the corner and henceforth, we will not discuss this matter," said Anurag.

On account of depression, I had to visit a doctor.

"Trauma has restricted the movement of life force from one to the other centre and caused the energy system to go haywire. He needs serious attention. He has become dormant," was the doctor's advice.

It was like...

The ice was here, the ice was there
the ice was all around.
It cracked and growled and roared and howled,
like noises in a sound!

Down dropped the breeze, the sail dropped down,
that was sad as sad could be;
and we did speak only to break
the silence of the sea!

About, about in real and rout,
the death flies danced at night.
The water like a witch's oil,
burnt green, and blue and white.

The ice of Samuel Taylor had become my tears. I recited many prayers in praise of God, but nothing happened.

Last time when I had seen her, she simply radiated with glow despite absolute simplicity. Her hair was free-flowing which added to her beauty.

My love for her is boundless. I love her unconditionally. If the situation warrants, I'll be manqué.

My friends asked me to get control over my life. According to them this period of transition may provide bliss, a life without worries. But I felt joyous only with memories of Shikha; everything else was useless for me.

All my talents had gone in vain. I felt worthless. Every night I went to sleep, hoping that Shikha would return to my life. I couldn't live without her; she was in my spirits.

For me, there is no heaven, no hell, no liberation! Nothing but love in this expanded cosmic consciousness.

Living is an art, a skill, a technique but I have lost pleasure in action and try to find peace and happiness by abstaining from peace and action. There is scarcely anyone who does not yearn for peace, but for me, there is no action, no peace.

To analyse, investigate and realise the quintessence of life and love, one should not submit oneself to blind faith, superstitious belief or mechanical rituals. My love is indelible; so, why this abstinence?

I know she loves me; she knows I love her. What she used to call 'a true love', I used to savour with her but now has begun my saturnine life without her. Was my love a fiasco? When love has no barriers, why is one afraid of this mundane barrier? Need I assure her that my love is not in the least affected by the increased distance between us? My love had never been salacious or amorous; it was gospel and devout. To marry her would have been the ultimate culmination, a blessing in disguise. She was the subsistence of my life. Without her, life is desolate. Only she can help me recuperate from the trauma I'm currently undergoing.

I am desperately waiting....

> *It will be easy to forget you....*
> *I just can't look at the sky*
> *or even remember the sea...*
> *I'll just have to stop dreaming*
> *and learn how to be alone...*
> *I know I'll forget you...*

I just can't remember your smile...
   your beautiful eyes,
your sweet voice...
   I can do it,
I know I can...

I just can't look to anything,
   I just can't remember,
I just can't live...
   or love...

I'll forget how important you have been in my life...
   I'll just have to forget myself...

The character "Pankaj" has abandoned himself from mundane matters
    due to excruciating circumstances.
    The despondent soul is lonely without love...

If Shikha loves Pankaj...then why is she reluctant to carry out relationship?
    Is it (love) ignoble and illusory?
    What will Pankaj do in this perplexed & imbroglio situation?

Has Shikha betrayed.....???

This story cannot end here...
Saga of love is indicating evocative scenes of hubbub and excitement...

Wait for the next part...